W0246663

Sleepytime Tales with CURIOUS CURIE

Sonia Mehta

Illustrated by Sunayana Nair

PUFFIN BOOKS

An imprint of Penguin Random House

PUFFIN BOOKS

USA | Canada | UK | Ireland | Australia
New Zealand | India | South Africa | China | Singapore

Puffin Books is part of the Penguin Random House group of companies
whose addresses can be found at global.penguinrandomhouse.com

Published by Penguin Random House India Pvt. Ltd
4th Floor, Capital Tower 1, MG Road,
Gurugram 122 002, Haryana, India

First published in Puffin Books by Penguin Random House India 2022

Text, design and illustrations copyright © Quadrum Solutions Pvt. Ltd 2022
Series copyright © Penguin Random House India 2022

All rights reserved

10 9 8 7 6 5 4 3 2

ISBN 9780143455400

Design and layout by Quadrum Solutions Pvt. Ltd

Printed at Repro India Limited

This book is sold subject to the condition that it shall not, by way of trade
or otherwise, be lent, resold, hired out, or otherwise circulated without the
publisher's prior consent in any form of binding or cover other than that in
which it is published and without a similar condition including this condition
being imposed on the subsequent purchaser.

www.penguin.co.in

MEET
CURIOUS CURIE
THE LITTLE SCIENTIST

She's super curious about everything.

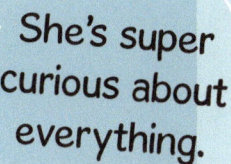

She's always on the lookout for answers about how the world works.

Psst! She has a superpower. She can talk to animals and plants.

MEET HUBBLE, CURIE'S BEST BUDDY.

Wherever Curie goes, Hubble follows her.

Curious Curie was wide awake. She had read three books, but was still wide awake.

She had counted hundreds of stars, but was still wide awake.

'Hubble,' she whispered to the faithful little dog who was always by her side.

'Hmfhh!' Hubble grunted, opening one eye.

'Are you awake?' whispered Curie in animal language. Remember, Curie could talk to animals though she was human.

'Why are you whispering?' grumbled Hubble. 'You woke me up just as I was dreaming about a yummy bone.'

'I can't sleep,' said Curie. 'Want to go for a walk?'

Hmfhh!

Hubble groaned. When Curie decided to do something, Hubble always agreed. Even though he sometimes thought Curie was as crazy as the next-door cat who loved yucky spinach.

'Okay, okay,' Hubble stretched and yawned. He jumped out of his little basket.

'Let's go to the forest,' suggested Curie. 'There will be things we'll spot at night that we never get to see in the day.'

'We'll just see everyone fast asleep, like we should be too,' Hubble grumbled. But he trotted along anyway.

'Let's follow that track,' said Curie pointing to a track, where the moonlight didn't quite reach.

'Why that way?' protested Hubble. 'Let's stay on the path where it's bright.'

'Don't be so boring,' said Curie. 'I'm sure we'll find something we've never seen before.' They stumbled along the rough track. Suddenly, Curie stopped.

'Hubble, did you hear that?' she said. There was a crackle and a sniffle.

'Who's that?' Curie called out. Hubble sniffed around. Who was crying in the middle of the forest, so late at night?

'It's me, Bushy, the squirrel,' a quivering voice said. 'I was collecting nuts when I fell into this silly hole. I've hurt my foot and can't move.'

'Oh dear!' exclaimed Curie. 'We'll help you. But it's dark and we can't see you.'

Just then, there was a whooshing sound.

'What do we have here?' a deep voice asked. It was Hoot, the owl.

'Bushy is hurt,' replied Curie. 'But why are you awake?'

'Ha ha ha ha!' Hoot laughed. 'Don't you know anything? I sleep all day and come out at night. I can see better at night.'

'That's good to know!' exclaimed Curie. 'Can you see Bushy in that hole?'

Hoot peered into the hole. 'Just about. But I can't get her out!'

'We must do something,' cried Curie. 'We can't leave her hurt like that.'

'Relax,' said Hoot. 'I'll call the Night Patrol.'

HOOOOOOOOT...

Hubble pricked up his ears.
The Night Patrol? That sounded fun!

'What's the Night Patrol?' asked Curie
curiously.

'You're not the only one wandering about
at night.' Hoot grinned. 'There are many
of us. We have the forest to ourselves
when everyone else is asleep,' Hoot gave
out a loud 'hoooooooooot'.

Suddenly, Curie heard soft footsteps.
To her astonishment, a group of animals
appeared.

'Meet the Night Patrol,' said Hoot.
'We sleep all day and wander around at
night. They call us NOCTURNAL animals.'

'This is Stripes, the badger.' Stripes
nodded his head shyly.

'This is Luna, the fox.' Luna waved her bushy tail.

'This is Pokey, the porcupine.' Pokey shook a quill.

'This is Wing, the bat.' Wing grumbled . He wasn't pleased that his hunting had been disturbed.

'And this,' continued Hoot, '. . . is Curie. She is a human. But she can speak our language.'

13

'I'm delighted to meet you all,' said Curie. 'Now, how shall we rescue poor Bushy?'

'I'll dig and make that hole wider,' said Stripes, the badger. 'I'm a good digger.'

'I'll climb down and push her up,' said Luna, the fox. 'I'm very nimble.'

'I'll hover on top and guide you,' said Wing, the bat. 'I'm smart.'

'I'll keep enemies at bay,' said Pokey, the porcupine. 'My sharp quills will protect us.'

'And I'll reach down and yank her up, with my long arms,' exclaimed Curie. Hubble sighed. *It was going to be a long night!*

'But I still can't see her properly like some of you can,' said Curie. 'It's too dark.'

Suddenly, a glow of light moved towards them.

'The fireflies!' exclaimed Hoot. 'They're part of our Night Patrol too.'

A swarm of sparkling fireflies hovered over the hole, casting a lovely soft light all around.

'Hello, fireflies,' said Curie, clapping. 'Thank you for the light.'

The Night Patrol got into action. Stripes, the badger, made the hole wider. Luna, the fox, climbed down and pushed Bushy up. And Curie yanked her out of the hole. Wing, Hoot and Pokey stood guard.

'Oh, thank you!' Bushy said happily.
'Now I can get home and fix my foot.'
She limped off.

'That was cool,' exclaimed Curie.
'I'm glad I couldn't fall asleep. We
wouldn't have met you all, otherwise.'

Hoot, Wing, Luna, Pokey and Stripes said
bye to Curie. They went off to wander
the forest till it was morning again.

'Shall we go home now?' asked Hubble.
'You know that we aren't nocturnal
animals, right? We need to be in bed.'
He was very sleepy.

Curie waved goodbye
to her new nocturnal
buddies as she and
Hubble made their
way home.

Soon, Curie was in bed with Hubble curled up in his basket.

'Wasn't that a lovely adventure, Hubble?' Curie asked sleepily. 'I had no idea there are so many creatures that stay awake all night.'

'Hmmmm,' Hubble mumbled, already half asleep.

'The next time I can't fall asleep, it'll be nice to know so many creatures are wide awake like me, right Hubble?' asked Curie.

But there was no reply. Hubble was fast asleep. Soon Curie's eyes closed. There was no sound. Except for the murmurs of the creatures of the night.

Curious Curie was excited. She was going deep-sea diving with her little dog Hubble for the very first time!

'Let's go to the beach, Hubble,' Curie said, in the special language in which she talked to animals.

Curie put on her wetsuit. She then put Hubble's breathing apparatus on.

'It's time to go deep-sea diving!'
she yelled.

Down, down, down went Curie and
Hubble, right to the seabed. It looked
like there was an enchanted garden at
the bottom of the sea.

23

'Look at those gorgeous flowers,' Curie said to Hubble. 'I wish we could plant them in our garden.'

'Those aren't flowers,' a deep voice suddenly boomed. Curie and Hubble looked around in surprise. A strange looking creature with wide wings, like an aeroplane, floated up.

'Are you a fish?' Curie asked curiously.

'I'm Flap, the stingray,' said the creature.
'I could sting you, but you look kind, so
I won't. Those *flowers* are corals. They
are animals like us all.'

Corals are animals? Curie and Hubble
couldn't believe that!

25

Just then, a school of tiny fish
swam out from behind the corals.
They swam together in a pattern,
as if they were one body.

'Wow, look at those fish swim in a
perfect pattern! Are they tied together?'
Curie asked awestruck.

Flap laughed. 'No, they aren't tied together. But some of us like to stay in groups,' Flap began to point out different types of fish.

'That one there is a puffer fish,' he said. 'It can blow itself out into a balloon to hide from big fish who might want to eat it.'

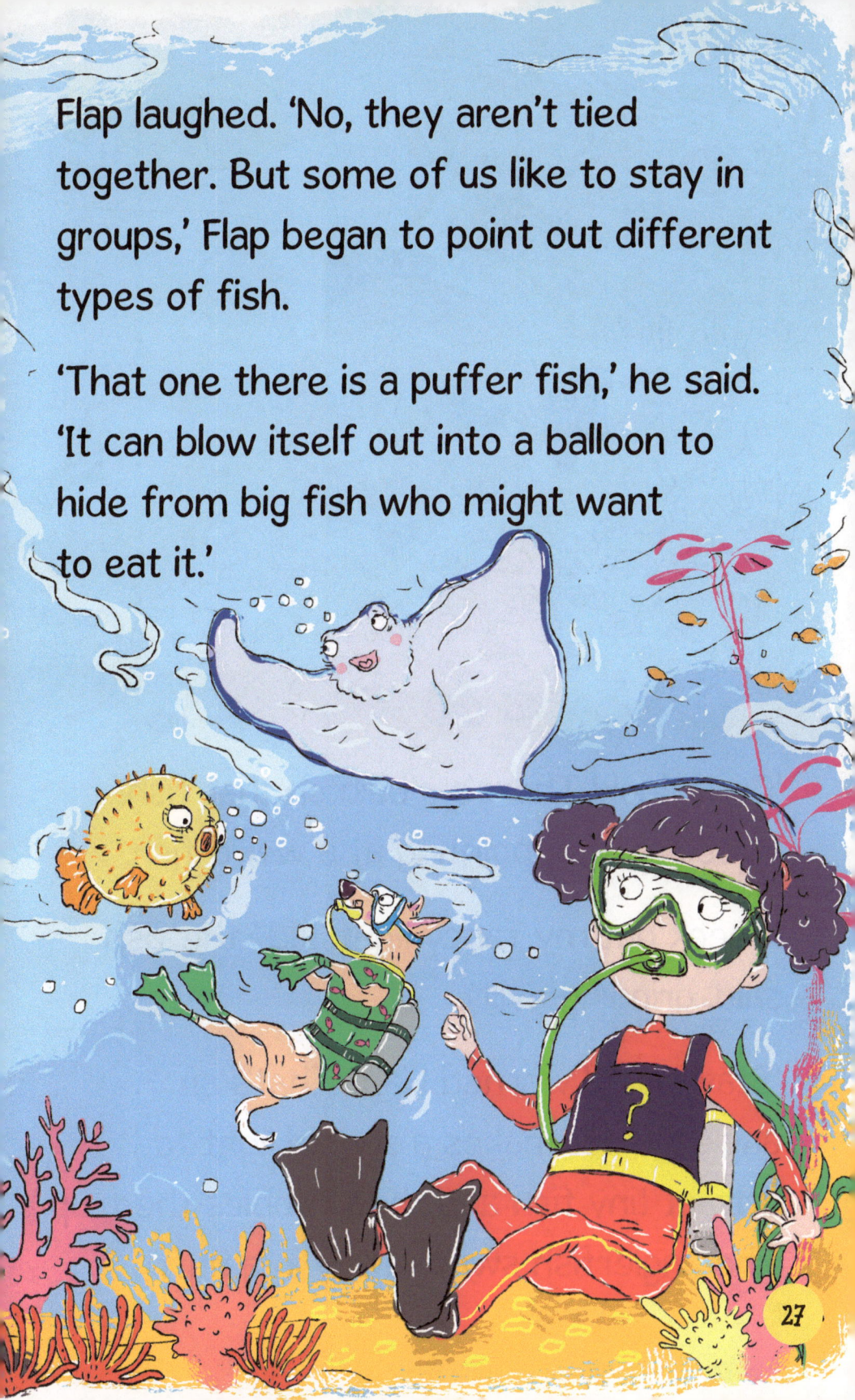

'Curie, look! There's a bulb on that fish!'
Hubble yelled, pointing at a weird fish.

'Check out my fancy light, kid,' the fish
said, grinning evilly.

'Stay away,' warned Flap. 'That's an
anglerfish. It makes a special light to
attract tiny fish and then gobbles them up.'
The anglerfish swam away in a huff.

Flap pointed out many strange fish. Colourful parrotfish, tiny sea horses, dotted yellow boxfish. Fish that crawled on the seabed, fish that darted about and fish that floated in the same spot.

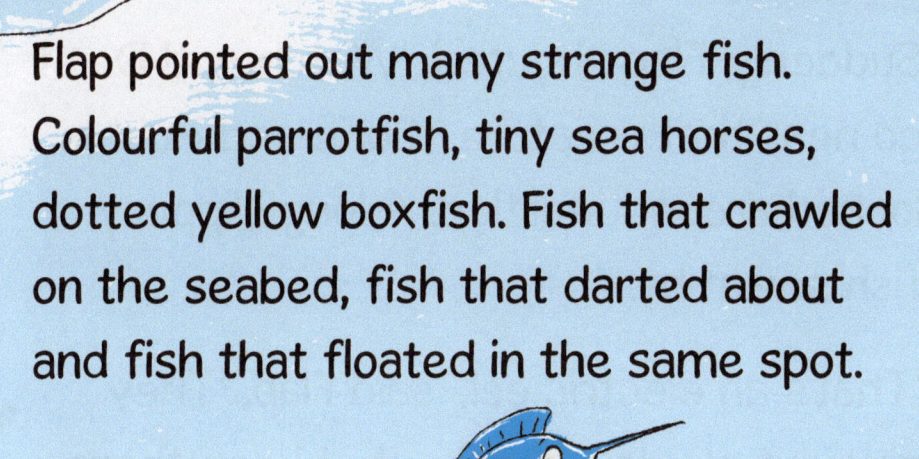

Suddenly, Flap shouted. 'Watch out! Don't go near that creature.' Curie and Hubble looked around startled. A long slippery fish swam by.

'That's an electric eel,' said Flap. 'They give out electric shocks that keep them safe from danger.'

All of a sudden, the water around them began to move in ripples. All the fish disappeared. Even Flap began to swim away.

'Wait, Flap,' called out Curie.

'Can't. The killer shark is coming,' shouted Flap. 'You had better hide too.'

Curie and Hubble rushed to hide behind a huge rock. A scary shark appeared. It had sharp teeth, like knives. It nosed around, looking for fish to gobble up. But there wasn't a single fish to be seen. Curie and Hubble stayed still.

Soon, the shark turned around
and swam off, disappointed.

Curie heaved a sigh of relief.

'Whew! That was close,' she said.
And then, she stared in shock.

A stone, that lay among the shells on the seabed, suddenly began to swim away.

'T-t-t-that stone is moving,' Curie said to Hubble, looking scared.

'Look,' said Hubble pointing. 'That bit of seaweed looks like it is swimming away too.'

'And what is that?' Curie shouted.
The sand on the seabed seemed to
be moving on its own.

'Ha ha ha ha,' they heard someone laugh.
Flap, the stingray was back. 'Those are
fish that have camouflaged themselves
so the shark doesn't spot them.'

'What's camouflage?' asked Curie, puzzled.

'Many of us change our appearance to match our surroundings,' explained Flap. 'That way bigger fish can't catch us, and we stay safe.'

'That is a stonefish pretending to be a stone,' he added. 'And that seaweed is actually a leafy sea dragon.'

'And what about that thing that was moving on the sand?' asked Hubble.

'That is a flatfish,' explained Flap. 'It takes on the colour of the sand so the shark can't spot it.'

Finally it was time for Curie and Hubble
to return home.

'Thank you for showing us around, Flap,'
said Curie to their new friend. Flap
waved goodbye with his large fins
and swam away.

Soon, they were back on the beach.

But where was Hubble? Suddenly, a mound of sand started moving. Two eyes popped out. And a wagging tail appeared.

'I was trying to camouflage myself,' grinned Hubble. *This was a fun trick to play*, he thought as he trotted home with Curie.

Curie and Hubble were on a long, long hike. Hubble was exhausted. He hated hikes, but wherever Curie went, he had to follow.

'Let's stop for a bit,' pleaded Hubble. They were walking up a slope and Hubble was quite out of breath.

'My legs are shorter than yours, remember?' he grumbled.

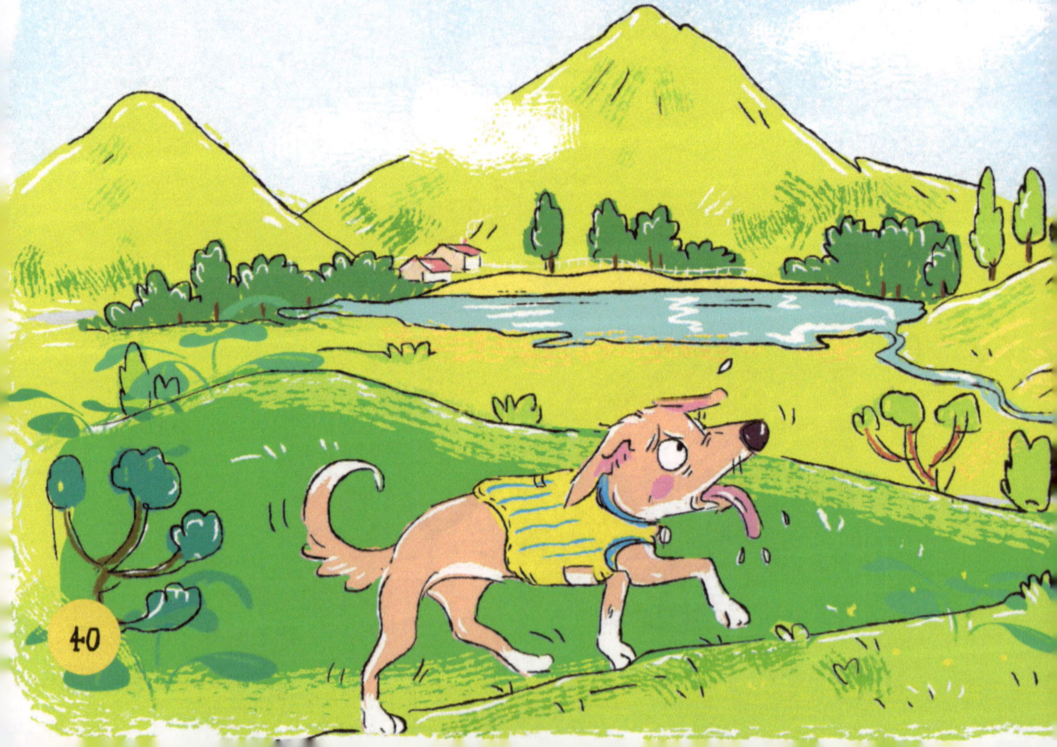

'Oh, come on, Hubble,' encouraged Curie. 'You can have orange crunchies when we're home.'

Hubble pricked up his ears. He loved orange crunchies. So, on he trudged tempted by the treat.

Curie and Hubble walked past an odd-looking house. It had flat, window-like panels on top. And it looked as if the house was built upside down.

Suddenly, Curie stopped.

'Did you hear that?' she asked looking around. 'Someone's calling my name.'

'Curieeeee, Curieeee,' a soft voice cried out. Curie and Hubble looked around.

A row of flowers seemed to be calling out to Curie.

She stopped and looked at the flowers. They were drooping sadly. The soil around them was dry and cracked.

'Hello,' she said. 'Why are you all looking so ill?'

'Oh, Curie,' cried a shrivelled rose. 'You must help us. We are dying because Zepo never waters us. We're so thirsty.'

'Zepo owns this house,' explained a dried sunflower. 'He spends all his time working on his computer and forgets to water us.'

'Everyone says that Zepo is smart,' explained the rose. 'He does something on his computer that he says can make life easier for humans.'

'But what about us?' wailed a withering petunia. 'He doesn't even remember to water us.'

'And he blocks out all our sunlight too,' grumbled the snapdragon.

'Well, first let's get you some sunlight and water,' said Curie briskly.

She replanted the flowers on the other side of the house, where the sun shone all day, and watered them thoroughly.

'Now let's get to the bottom of what this Zepo is up to,' she said, marching up to the door of the strange house.

KNOCK! KNOCK! KNOCK!

A funny looking man opened the door. His hair was messy. His shirt was crumpled, and he seemed to have spilled some jam on it.

'What can I do for you?' asked Zepo.

'Quite a lot,' said Curie sternly. 'Have you seen your flowers? They are dying of thirst and from lack of sunlight. And you don't seem to care.'

Zepo blinked. 'Dying? My flowers? I don't have any flowers!' he said, looking puzzled.

'Then what are those?' Curie demanded, pointing to the now perky flowers.

'Dear me! Are those my flowers?' Zepo asked in wonder.

'Why did you build a house that blocks out the sunlight for those poor flowers?' demanded Curie.

'I had to build the house this way so I could capture sunlight,' explained Zepo. 'See those panels on my roof? They are solar panels.'

'What are those?' asked Curie, puzzled.

Zepo invited Curie into his odd little house. Papers, wires and computers were strewn about higgledy-piggledy. Curie looked around, fascinated.

'I am trying to use the energy from the sun as electricity,' explained Zepo. 'The solar panels capture sunlight and turn it into energy. So instead of burning wood or building dams to get electricity, just the sun's heat can light up the village!'

'You mean the sun has enough energy to help us create electricity?' Curie asked Zepo, her mouth open in wonder.

'Oh yes,' said Zepo. 'All that heat and energy comes to us and just gets wasted.'

Curie looked gobsmacked. 'So we won't need to cut down trees, or dig for oil, or build dams to get electricity!' she exclaimed.

'That's right,' beamed Zepo, delighted that someone understood him.

Hubble pawed at Curie impatiently. He wanted to get home to his orange crunchies, but Curie just wouldn't stop talking to this weird-smelling man.

'Well, we must be off,' said Curie.
'Please build a solar panel for me too.
And don't forget to water your
flowers,' she said wagging a finger.

Curie waved goodbye to the flowers. 'I'm glad you stopped me,' she said. 'Now Zepo will make sure you have plenty of sunlight and water, won't you, Zepo?'

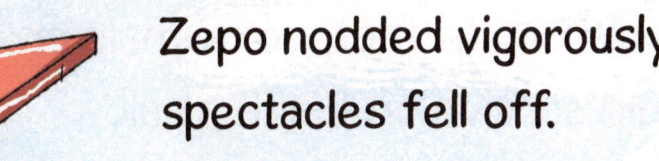

Zepo nodded vigorously till his spectacles fell off.

Hubble wagged his tail. At last, it looked like they were going home.

Curious Curie sat by the window. The sun was setting.

'Just imagine, Hubble,' she said. 'The sun is so important for us all. Without sunlight, all plants would die. In fact, no animals or humans would survive on Earth at all.'

'And with Zepo's solar panels, it will be the sunlight that will make this toaster work. Can you imagine that, Hubble?' she asked, gazing at the setting sun.

'Crrrrrunch crrrrrunch,' came the reply. Hubble was busy gobbling up his orange crunchies.

Crunch!
Crunch!

CURIE AND THE FALLING COCONUTS

It was the perfect day for a picnic by the lake. The sun was shining. Curie lazed on the picnic mat gazing up at the clouds, while Hubble dozed beside her.

'Did you know that there are four types of clouds, Hubble?' she said.

Hubble just grunted. Curie was about to describe each type of cloud when there was a loud shout.

'OUCH! OUCH! OUCH!' someone yelled. 'Drat these pesky coconuts. Always disturbing my sleep.'

Startled, Hubble jumped up. Curie looked around to see who was yelling.

It was Tonka the monkey, looking rather upset.

'What's wrong?' Curie asked the monkey, in the special language she used to speak to animals.

'I was fast asleep under this coconut tree, when this coconut plonked on my head,' Tonka grumbled. 'Wait, you silly coconut. I'm throwing you right back.'

Tonka picked up the coconut
and flung it upwards to the sky
with all his might.

up it went.

up

Up

And then . . .

CRASH!

Down down down it came.

CRASH! It landed right back on Tonka's head.

'Blistering bananas!' Tonka yelled, rubbing his head. 'How did you come back right at me?' he hollered, glaring at the coconut.

'Calm down, Tonka,' Curie said grinning. 'No matter how many times you throw the coconut in the air, it will come right back down. That's because of gravity.'

'Gra . . . what? What's that?' Tonka asked, looking confused.

'G-R-A-V-I-T-Y! Many years ago, a scientist called Newton was asleep under a tree,' explained Curie. 'An apple fell on his head, and that's when he discovered that there is a force called gravity.'

'I'm sure the apple didn't hurt as much as this dratted coconut,' grumbled Tonka. 'And what is gravity anyway?'

'There is a very, very strong force deep in the core of our Earth that pulls us all towards it,' explained Curie. 'That's why we stick to Earth and don't fall off.'

'That's silly,' exclaimed Tonka. 'We aren't stuck to Earth, like there's glue or something. See, I'll show you! I can jump from one tree to another as if I'm flying. I'm not stuck to anything.'

Tonka leapt nimbly from tree to tree. And then, oops!

He took a rather big leap, reached out to grab a branch . . . and missed.

THUD! Tonka landed on the ground.

'Ow, that hurts!' hollered Tonka, rubbing his sore backside. But he was still not convinced.

'I fell because I missed the branch,' he said. 'It had nothing to do with gravity!'

'Then why didn't you float off into the sky instead of falling down to the ground?' asked Curie with a grin.

'Ummmmmm,' Tonka began to think. He had no answer.

'It was gravity that pulled you down,' explained Curie. 'Many planets have it. The sun does too.'

Just then, Squawk, the parrot, flew past.

'See!' said Tonka pointing to Squawk. 'Squawk isn't falling down. How come gravity isn't pulling her down?'

'Squawk's wings have a force called *lift*,' explained Curie, while Squawk looked curiously at her wings.

'Her wings overcome the force of gravity when she flaps them correctly. That's what makes her fly—like all birds. But if she didn't use her wings, she would fall, like you did.'

Squawk hopped off the branch. And sure enough, she fell instead of flying off.

THUD!

'See, Tonka?' said Curie. 'If Squawk doesn't flap her wings, the force of gravity will pull her to Earth, just like it pulls us!'

'Well, maybe you are right,' Tonka said. 'Let me check.'

He picked up a large pebble and flung it towards the lake. First it went upwards. And then down it came and SPLASHED into the water, drenching poor Hubble who was trying to have a nap.

'Ummm, okay,' said Tonka finally. 'I believe you. But what would happen if there was no gravity?' he wondered, scratching his head.

'Everything would just float away,' replied Curie. 'Like it does in outer space.'

'You mean we would just float around?' exclaimed Tonka. 'What fun!'

'It won't be fun if your food floats away and you can't catch it,' giggled Curie.

Hubble opened one eye. It didn't sound fun to him either.

'Well, it's time we went home,' said Curie. She and Hubble packed up their picnic things and off they went.

Later that night, Curie looked up at the night sky in wonder.

'Hubble, would you like to float around without gravity?' she asked sleepily.

Hubble snuggled deeper into his blanket. Oh no! He was happy that gravity kept him and his beloved Curie firmly on Earth.